# HOW TO EVALUATE YOUR OWN WRITING

## Editing Made Easy

For information address:

Karen Venable
P.O. Box 741623
Dallas, Texas 75374
pes1210@aol.com.

Library of Congress Cataloging-in-Publication Data

Karen Venable Evaluating

Your Own Writing: Editing

Made Easy

ISBN 978-1-935451-14-3

Library of Congress Control Number: 2010927706

First Edition

# HOW TO EVALUATE YOUR OWN WRITING
## EDITING MADE EASY

*For all of those writers who have fought the battle and felt the ecstasy.*

**Before You Begin Writing**

What is your psychological makeup? Who are you? These questions are necessary because it is important for you to be sure about the type of writing you are trying to create. Are you interested in thrillers, mysteries, literary, historical, romance, erotic, horror, sci-fi, etc.? In order to find out where your passion lies, you must be able to look at yourself objectively. What are the social practices that you feel comfortable with? What are the social practices that you are uncomfortable with? Are you comfortable writing an erotic book, or a violent thriller or a romance novel? If you are a non-drinker, would it be possible for you to create a believable three-dimensional character that is an alcoholic? Are you an evangelical, agnostic, Catholic or an atheist? Could you craft a novel about only religious people or by non-religious characters? These are just a few reasons why it is important to recognize what your comfort zones are.

## You Write With Your Brain

Our brains conjure up the mental images that we wish to write about. It is a data bank containing images that the writer can inject into his or her prose. Good imagery enables the writer to transport readers to exotic places and introduce them to compelling characters. Writers who are able to conjure up emotions such as love, hate, anger, jealously, depression, ect., build memorable characters that come alive for the reader.

## Lock In Your Reader at the Get-go

Here are five things you need to convey at the very beginning of your book.

1) Who is the hero, the protagonist? In other words, whose book is it?
2) Are your characters fully fleshed out?
3) Have you created enough dramatic tension to impel the reader to keep reading?
4) What is going on in the story? Does it flow?
5) Is your writing well-edited?

The first line of a novel is all-important. This sentence sets the tone and contains the implication of the rest of the novel. The first paragraph must continue this idea of implying something that will be examined throughout the work; a theme, idea, conviction, etc.

## Overwriting and Showing Not Telling

A common mistake that most writers make is to overwrite, not allowing their scenes to speak through context, implication, mood, etc., and to "tell, not show." When authors tell their readers what they should know (instead of having the reader feel it, know it implicitly through the action and scene) they reduce their characters to two dimensional cutouts. If, for example, the author goes on and on about how angry one of his or her characters is, then that is all the reader will know. The trick is making the reader feel the anger through implication, dialogue and actions. When this happens the author's work approaches art.

Remember this well. When writing a novel, you must show action, craft compelling dialogue, and become invisible to the reader. In other words, when you catch yourself overwriting, less is invariably more. Subtlety, understatement, implication, and multiple meanings work wonders to build a narrative that is multi-layered and full of depth.

Writing is much like the human body. You begin with a skeleton. This is your foundation, the thing that your entire story rests upon. At this point, your story will need a lot of editing. A good exercise is to try and write without adjectives and adverbs. This way, your sentences will become stronger, using only adjectives and adverbs when necessary. Next, you will have to put in the muscle, not any fat. Keep your manuscript lean. What follows is the skin, the imagery of your manuscript. It is the rich patina that will help make your manuscript sing. After you've crafted your body, it's time to edit, edit, edit. Cut out any extraneous sections. If you see areas where you have overwritten, cut it down. Remember, when it comes to overwriting, less is more.

## Telling Not Showing

The shock of life in the New World was hard on immigrants, and my father's family was no exception.

## Showing Not Telling

The smell of horse manure rivaled that of freshly baked bread. The streets were of dirt, and sometimes of mud, in the Little Italy of 1927, where I played my first game of baseball, and first heard of the Babe.

When you *show* instead of *tell*, you might not say anything. But, you have set the scene for what is to come. Just by letting the story unfold, you allow the life of the immigrant in 1920s New York be revealed.

## Avoiding Basic Errors

Two most common errors for beginning writers:

a)  Overwriting emotion
b)  Underwriting prose

When we overwrite emotion, we attempt to push our readers into feeling what we want them to feel. Sorry, it can't be done. You must learn how to let the scene play itself out on the page. If the scene is compelling, it will have the desired effect on the reader. If not, then no amount of narrative hand-wringing will help. To improve on your own skills, read scenes by exceptional authors. Read how 'Doc' dies in William Goldman's *Marathon Man*. The last two words, you will always remember. Writing emotion requires great discipline or it becomes sappy.

## Example of keeping emotion in check

Katheryn took several steps and froze. The baby's small head protruded from Jacqueline's open womb. The sight branded itself on her soul.

*Dear Father in Heaven*

Sinking to her knees, Katheryn crawled over to Jacqueline's body and covered it with the torn nightgown.

Watchman Choy touched her shoulder. "Missee, you come with me. This place no good."

Katheryn stared at her bloody hands, knowing she had just been baptized into the world of man.

Underwriting is less common than overwriting, but here the beginning writer confuses underwriting with lean prose, such as the brilliant phrasing by John D. MacDonald which conveys images in simple, well-turned phrases that have momentum and conjure images. Underwriting prose leaves gaps in the continuity of the story. The reader has to search about, trying to plug something in to bridge the gap. If you have this problem, you might want to show it to a qualified editor to help get you on the right track.

## Example of Less is Best

After seeing that Jacqueline's body was properly attended, Katheryn went upstairs to Marianne's room. The bed was unmade. A stuffed bear with a red ribbon around its neck lay on the pillow. She went to the window and stared down at the dark courtyard. Tong-Po, almost invisible in the shadows, was issuing instructions to the men.

Turning, her gaze took in the room. *A child's room, with Jacqueline's loving touches everywhere.*

Katheryn saw a small envelope tucked beneath the bear's arm. She sat down, opened the envelope, and removed the card.

*For my little princess.*

*I love you,*

*Daddy.*

Katheryn slipped the card back inside the envelope and stared at the darkness outside the window. There were no tears. They would come later, or perhaps never.

## Adjective Overload

New writers usually commit one common error. They tend to construct weak sentences, then try to strengthen them by filling them up with an abundance of adjectives and adverbs. This technique will not work. The best thing to do to improve one's writing is to practice writing without adjectives and adverbs. This way, the strength of your sentence must come from its innate structure. After doing this every day for three or four months, allow yourself one adjective and one adverb before writing something. You will be amazed at how carefully you will dole out your two freebies. You'll guard them jealously; you'll use them with care and precision. This, of course, is what we should have done in the first place.

## A Novel's Shape

Well-written novels have a shape like a mountain. As the story unfolds, the reader climbs the mountain over numerous switchbacks, rough terrain, and impediments before reaching the summit, the climax. There must be plenty of obstacles along the ascent. These hazards need to be of a dangerous nature, in order for the journey to be of a dangerous nature, in order for the journey to be interesting and compelling to the reader.

In a not-so-well-written book, readers follow the path of a long, well-traveled, mountain road. It takes the reader slowly and steadily to the top with no bumps along the way. This novel lacks serious conflict. The reader instinctively knows that the character(s) will eventually reach the summit. It will just take a long time.

The final shape of a novel takes place in the desert. The desert may be beautiful to the eye, but the reader is not aware of any life struggles taking place beyond the windshield. The landscape is flat, devoid of any dynamic tension, which would contribute to the novel and give it the kind of life that would make it memorable. Instead, this might be a well-written novel that didn't go anywhere, populated by characters who never experience real change.

## Dialogue

A common mistake with dialogue is to overwrite. In this case, the author provides too many unnecessary details, all of which can be removed without hurting the plot. It is important for you to remember that your characters are yours to command, to take the story in the direction you want it to go. It is imperative that what the characters say and do be important to furthering the narrative.

When crafting your dialogue, remember less is invariably more. In conversation, people generally don't say what they mean. The true meaning is contained in an undercurrent, an implied silence of gestures, intonation, and body language. This is commonly known as subtext. However, since you can't rely on body language and gestures as you would in a film, you must convey the "unsaid" primarily through mood and tone. A good example of this kind of writing is in the movie *"Tortilla Soup."* The dialogue is mainly ordinary interactions between family members, but a world of things are implied in the dialogue itself and in the responses of the characters to each other.

Another common mistake is to make the dialogue overly formal and stilted, as if the characters exist only to say what you, as the author, want them to say. This eliminates any kind of surprises, makes the prose seem flat, and the characters not human or believable. Readers must be convinced that your characters are real, living, breathing human beings with histories, conflicting emotions, and complex motivations. Let the scenes of dialogue breathe. Give the characters some room and they'll come alive and surprise you, the reader as well. Instead of your characters all just saying things directly the first time out of the blocks, let them go at their own pace, in their own idiosyncratic way. Let them meander and digress, providing that these digressions are loaded with subtext, and shine a light on the narrative and further it along.

Watch out for inner monologues. These should be kept at a minimum for maximum effect. Readers should feel, think, understand, and wonder about what's happening through implication, instead of through you, the author, stating it in no uncertain terms. You want your readers to experience your book firsthand; you want them to feel what the characters feel, instead of just being told what they are not doing distances the reader from your book and allows them to lose interest. Inner monologues should be a conduit to the soul of the novel, not a substitute or a reiteration, of action.

## Tension and Contrast

In literature, trouble is interesting, not happiness. Tension is what propels a story—tension and its eventual release. The hero must overcome insurmountable odds, and hurdle epic impediments in order to reach his goal. *Romeo Juliet* would not work if they both came from loving, supportive families, who were actually neighbors and best friends and had meals together every weekend. Instead, there must be turmoil, strife, and unrest. People and events must arise to thwart the hero, so that the reader will want to step in and intervene.

A devil's advocate is a great convention, because it works to point out the hero's fallibility and creates tension by showing where the hero is and where he should be. Build tension and contrast through character, scene, and dialogue. Do not diffuse it with asides that reroute the narrative, or with too many details about situations and characters that aren't important to the story.

Remember that people generally like a quick read. Get off with a good first sentence, your hook, then keep it moving at a good pace. Close out your chapter with a sentence that makes your reader want to go to the next chapter. Here again, you must look critically at what successful authors have done. Thrillers always have a good kicker.

## Ah, The Hero

The protagonist of a novel has a number of requirements.

1) They must elicit sympathy from the reader. Even antagonists must have something about them that is compelling.

2) Heroes must have difficult, complex obstacles to overcome.

3) Heroes, throughout the course of the novel, must change in some way. They cannot remain static.

The substance of most novels is the hero's struggle, his quest. Therefore, heroes must eventually be proactive. They must be responsible for their own destiny. If the hero or heroine are too passive throughout the book, they become pathetic and no longer the hero. This will cause the reader to withdraw support.

## Enter The Villain

The villain, or antagonist, must be formidable. In the world of villains, there is no room for the milquetoast, the wishy- washy. Their character must be drawn in such a way that the reader believes them fully capable of anything. By doing this, the tension is maintained throughout the course of the novel, and it is left in doubt, until the end, as to whether or not the villain will vanquish the hero. Formidability, a methodical nature, and relentlessness are hallmarks of the successful villain. A common mistake made by beginning writers is to not fully commit to their antagonist, perhaps out of fear of delving too deeply into his dark side. Too often their villains end up being fallible, inept, or downright incompetent, which is like removing the fangs from a snake. In a serious novel, this is disastrous. It makes the villains seem comic, ludicrous. The protagonist depends on the antagonist for his eventual growth and any epiphanies he might have. Consequently, the greater the villain, the greater the hero's triumph (if in the end he surmounts the antagonist and succeeds).

Check out some of the great villains in literature as models. Shakespeare's Richard III was a very treacherous villain. Macbeth, who begins as the hero, then, with a little help from his wife, transforms into a fiend.

Wolf Larsen, from Jack London's *The Sea Wolf,* is about as formidable and malevolent a villain as you can get.

## The Work

Fiction writers must take great pains to make sure their characters are believable, so the reader sees them as living, breathing human beings, with living histories that inform their actions with contradictory emotions, moral ambiguities, and complex motivations. The writer must probe the depths of their characters to find the organic, the intrinsic, the qualities which separate them from the "stock characters," the stereotypes, in order to give them their own unique lives. Keeping this approach in mind, it would be a disservice to just slap on some arbitrary job. Too often, writers assign a job to a character simply because the character must, after all, do something. So, they become a doctor, lawyer, an Indian chief, without any regard to who they really are, and the kind of job they would naturally get for themselves. For the character's work to be anything more than window dressing, the job must be a logical result of the character's organic, intrinsic nature. Only then will it be believable, and add to the narrative.

## Sex and Violence Scene Example

Violent and erotic scenes can be boring and tedious. The trick is making these scenes unique. It should not follow the standard stereotypical scenes found in romance novels. Make it believable, so the reader can visualize the actual characters performing the sexual or violent act.

Example: Eric opened his eyes and found Katheryn standing at the end of the tub. She wore a red silk robe tied at the waist, her hair falling about her shoulders in golden ringlets. Her eyes grew luminous as she untied the sash of her robe. Parting, it hung momentarily like butterfly wings, then drifted to the floor. Katheryn watched his eyes as his gaze explored the landscape of her body.

The faint scent of her perfume came to him. His wife had never looked so beautiful to him as she did now.

Katheryn realized her life had been lived inside some sort of puritanical Victorian dream. *Ahh, but it's so nice to be awake,* she thought. Moving forward, she slipped into the tub, resting her head at the opposite end. Her toes brushed his thigh—then their legs were intertwined.

Eric watched his wife's hair fan around her.

## Violent Scene

The assassin uncoiled and dropped silently to a spot on the floor about ten paces behind Eric. He crouched and froze. Eric's head did not move. He drew a thin-bladed knife and crept forward.

Perhaps it was the slightest rustle of fabric, or some primal sense that made Eric turn around. His eyes locked with the assassin's. Then he was being attacked. Candlelight glinted off polished steel. Eric moved as the knife whistled through the air. The razor-shapr blade sliced his shoulder as he pushed himself to the other side of the tub.

The assassin leapt in after him. Eric whirled to meet the onrush. The knife arched again, only this time Eric stepped in, with an upward thrust of his forearm, blocking the blow. Twisting his hand, he locked onto the assailant's wrist. Anticipating such a defense, the assassin stiffened his fingers, striking at Eric's midsection. He sank to the edge of the tub, but somehow maintained his grip on the assassin's wrists.

The aberration loomed above Eric, the knife at his eye. Relentless downward pressure propelled the blade forward. Soft laughter from behind the mask. "Soon now."

An ear-shattering report rocked the room. There was a shower of blood as the assassin's hood flew off.

Eric looked up and saw Katheryn framed against the door. Her body shook. Killing another human being was an act she had not dreamt possible, but she felt no remorse. She would kill again and again, a thousand times again, if it meant protecting Eric's life. The stink of gunpowder was strong. Her pistol still aimed at the lifeless form floating beside him.

Watchman Choy arrived a moment later. "Where you want us to take body, Taipan?"

Katheryn slipped out of Eric's arms. "Don't bury it. Take it to Bartrum and Sons and tie it to the front gate."

**First scene** gets the point across that they're naked and about to have sex. It also provides a lot of subtext. They are man and wife, but the wife is just now breaking out of her Victorian roots. Katheryn has never looked more beautiful to Eric. They are about to grow closer as man and wife.

**Second scene** solidifies their relationship. Katheryn kills the assassin sent to murder her husband. Although the thought of killing another human being was abhorrent to her, she would do it over and over again to protect her husband. They have grown both mentally and intimately closer.

## Contradictions

Contradictions and paradox are useful in helping develop characters by making them more human. The author's task is to let their readers know that they are aware of the contradictions. For example, the author might have described a CIA agent or business mogul as tough as nails on page 20. Later, on page 65, the reader learns that CIA agent is afraid to go back into the field, or that the business mogul doesn't want to face his board of directors. The use of contradictions allows the reader to recognize that the protagonist has all too human qualities as part of his character.

## Characters

It is vital that you make your characters distinctive. If they all are attractive and share the same opinions, it becomes boring for the reader. Also, do not populate the narrative with numerous characters unless they are all important, in that they further the narrative. Remember, if a character doesn't move the action/ story along, either condense him/her into a character who does, or eliminate them.

## Character Description

Do not just describe someone for the sake of describing. Do so in a way that provides telling details that makes him/her stand out, makes them unique, that sheds light on the character, and helps build the mood.

## Pretty Good

Eric Gradek's calm surprised many when he stepped out onto the balcony of the Commerce Club. He had been back from Chongming Dao for two days and rumors were rampant. A fortune in opium had been stolen from Dragon Mok and Alex Bartrum by Formidable Fung and an unknown barbarian.

## Good

Declining offers of conversation, Eric sipped hot tea alone on the Commerce Club balcony. His suit jacket and cravat hung over a nearby chair. His white shirt was unbuttoned at the neck, and his black leather boots were polished to a high gloss. Behind him the room buzzed with conversation.

## Character Development

This is what makes a character live, come alive, become a full-fledged, fleshed out human being, whom the reader cares about in some way. Hate or love, it doesn't matter, as long as the reader grants the character their existence. Otherwise, the character seems flat, two- dimensional, a caricature of a real person.

Character development is a matter of feel, of getting to know your character(s). It is the intrinsic sense we get of a person through long days spent in the quiet and exacting art of observation. What separates this character from everyone else? Obviously, you can assemble a list of qualities, quirks, and eccentricities that will help develop your characters. But, in so doing, you must be careful not to use the same ones that are commonly used in romance and mystery novels. You want to avoid having your characters come across as formulaic. (Example: Private detective's phone rings and he knocks his bottle of Jack Daniels on the floor as he reaches for the receiver.) (Romance novel: The young woman watched the man dismount from the black stallion, and start walking towards her. He was shirtless, his tanned muscular torso covered with a thin sheen of sweat.)

## Description of Action

Example:

Gloria ran outside, unlocked her car door, slipped inside, started the engine, locked the doors, backed out, and drove away.

Simplified by:

Gloria rushed to her car and drove away.

Another example:

"I'm going to the store," Jack said. He pulled his car keys out of his pocket, walked outside, opened his car door, got inside, backed out of the driveway and drove off.

Simplified by:

"I'm going to the store," Jack said. He walked out, got in his car and drove away.

## Narrative Voice

Here are some examples of narrative voice. It is acceptable for the author of a novel to engage readers through character and plot, but also through narrative voice. The narrative, of course, is the story, and the way the story is told is the narrative voice, which can also be thought of as "style." It can be prosaic and straightforward, relating things in sequence in a plain, unadorned style.

"There is an ecstasy that marks the summit of life, and beyond which life cannot rise. And such is the paradox of living, this ecstasy comes when one is most alive, and it comes as a complete forgetfulness that one is alive.

"This ecstasy, this forgetfulness of living, comes to the artist, caught up and out of himself in a sheet of flame; it comes to the soldier, war-mad in a stricken field and refusing quarter; and it came to Buck, leading the pack, sounding the old wolf-cry, straining after the food that was alive and that fled swiftly before him through the moonlight."

--Jack London, *Call of the Wild*

"In the late summer of that year we lived in a house in a village that looked across the river and the plain to the mountains. In the bed of the river there were pebbles and boulders, dry and white in the sun, and the water was clear and swiftly moving and blue in the channels."

--Ernest Hemingway, *A Farewell to Arms*

"Call me Ishmael. Some years ago—never mind how long precisely—having little or no money in my purse, and nothing particular to interest me on shore, I thought I would sail about a little and see the watery part of the world. It is a way I have of driving off the spleen, and regulating the circulation. Whenever I feel myself growing grim and out the mouth; whenever it is a damp, drizzly November in my soul "

--Herman Melville, *Moby Dick*

"The sky struck to them; the birds sang through them. And, what was even more exciting, she felt, too, as she saw Mr. Ramsay bearing down and retreating, and Mrs. Ramsay sitting with James in the window and the cloud moving and the tree bending, how life, for being made up of little separate incidents which one lived one by one, became curled and whole like a wave which bore one up with it and threw one down with it, there, with a dash on the beach."

--Virginia Woolf, *To the Lighthouse*

"Granted: I am an inmate of a mental hospital; my keeper is watching me, he never lets me out of his sight; there's a peephole in the door, and my keeper's eye is the shade of brown that can never see through a blue-eyed type like me."

--Gunter Grass, *The Tin Drum*

"But it did not all happen in a day, this giving over of himself, body and soul, to the man-animals. He could not immediately forego his wild heritage and his memories of the Wild. There were days when he crept to the edge of the forest and stood and listened to something calling him far and away."

--Jack London, *White Fang*

"I give you the mausoleum of all hope and desire . . . I give it to you not that you may remember time, but that you might forget it now and then for a moment and not spend all of your breath trying to conquer it. Because no battle is ever won he said. They are not even fought. The field only reveals to man his own folly and despair, and victory is an illusion of philosophers and fools."

--William Faulkner, *The Town: A Novel of the Snopes Family*

"Clocks slay time . . . time is dead as long as it is being clicked off by little wheels; only when the clock stops does time come to life."

--William Faulkner, *The Sound and the Fury*

"So we beat on, boats against the current, borne back ceaselessly into the past."

--F. Scott Fitzgerald, *The Great Gatsby*

"I'm not sentimental—I'm as romantic as you are. The idea, you know, is that the sentimental person thinks things will last—the romantic person has a desperate confidence that they won't."

--F. Scott Fitzgerald, *This Side of Paradise*

**Verisimilitude: the appearance or semblance of truth;**

**likelihood; probability.**

This is essential in all works of fiction. Simply put, the reader must accept the author's world, the context of reality that they create. Even in something like *Alice in Wonderland,* there must be an *intrinsic truth in context* which the reader will accept and believe, or at least be willing to suspend their disbelief.

If, for example, you cast your main character as a crackerjack, securities and exchange investigator, and it turns out he is taking bribes from powerful investment bankers, you will have to explain yourself to the reader or they will feel hoodwinked, betrayed. The bottom line is that the situations and characters you create must be believable in context.

## Passion vs. the Brass Tacks of Writing

*Passion* occurs when you are inexplicably seized by inspiration; touched by the Muse. Your words flow effortlessly, and you are the dam, barely able to hold them back. You put pen to paper, or fingers to keyboard, and just like that the dam overflows. Passion is the first part of creative writing. Here, it is implied that what you are writing about is worthy of the Muse's inspiration. As Herman Melville said, "To have a mighty book, you must have a mighty theme." An entire novel can be written under the spell of passion, but then the second part of creative writing must take place in order for the work to be complete.

*Brass Tacks* is the nuts and bolts of writing, the calm after the storm; when you look back objectively at what you've written with the sinister intention of hacking it to bits. As I've said before, it's better that you be ruthless in editing your own work. After you've finished, you might want a qualified editor to give a second opinion. It is best to have your work be as good as it can be before sending it out into the world, and this usually involves massive editing. Remember, you are not crossing out words and paragraphs for the sake of using the red pen, but rather in the hope of liberating your words and ideas. By finding and focusing on what's essential, your prose will shine out, unencumbered by the distractions that would have otherwise mired it down, and prevented the reader from seeing its beauty.

## Dialogue Exercises

Basically, there are two types of dialogue: The type used where we have characters confront each other, often with strong emotions; and the type where characters simply exchange information.

Try your hand at two pages of confrontational dialogue. Avoid telling the reader. Instead, remember always to show the reader what's happening through dialogue, actions and implication.

a.   Frank enters a room and sees his brother, Mark, for the first time in eleven years.
b.   Ashley, a brilliant concert pianist, must be told that her right hand needs to be amputated.
c.   Jack must ask his devoted wife, Sandy, for a divorce.

Try these information examples by having the two men talk in a natural way.

a.  Eric and Katheryn have just finished making love. The conversation is now focused on how Eric can extricate himself from being wiped out by his arch enemy Alex Bartrum, who is holding his notes. (Katheryn should have a lot of input.) Remember that Shanghai is a dangerous, rough and tumble place where men would lie, steal, cheat, and even kill to control the flow of oil into Asia.

b.  Grant Corbet walks into Zach Holden's office (his boss). He learns he's been tapped to track down an international assassin Basha, who has been executing prominent Jews around the world. Grant is afraid he will be the sacrificial lamb if he fails to capture or kill the assassin, with the presidential elections coming up.

## Creative Writing's Seven Phases

1)  Research, fact-finding, information gathering— nurturing and germinating ideas.
2)  Putting your ideas down on the page.
3)  Completing the first draft.
4)  Intensive editing.
5)  Editing slows down. You realize that writing is a particularly hard business. You begin to wonder if what you've written is any good.
6)  Editing smoothes out. You start going through the manuscript and begin making minor changes.
7)  Finished.

Once you are satisfied with your work, it is advisable to let a qualified editor give it a read through to make sure you are indeed ready to send your work out to agents and publishers.

## Query Letters

What each query letter should be:

1) Professional (includes SASE, is error free and addressed to the right editor).
2) New (idea is fresh, contemporary, and up front).
3) Provocative (opening pulls reader in).
4) Creative (presentation is off beat, new, and vibrant).
5) Focused (story narrowed down; length is kept to one page).
6) Customized (appropriate for certain trade publications or magazines).
7) Multifaceted (offers several options on how it could be marketed).
8) Realistic (inspires confidence that the project is doable).
9) Accredited (includes your clips, credits, and qualifications).
10) Conclusive (confirms that you're the best and only writer to do it).

What each query letter should not be:

1) Wordy (text rambles; length exceeds one and a half pages).
2) Sketchy (idea isn't fleshed out enough).
3) Presumptuous (tone is too cocky).

4) Egotistical (topic is about you).
5) Reluctant (lame reason about why you have written it).
6) Loose-lipped (article is offered on spec).
7) Stubborn (prior rejects by same editor haven't given you the hint).
8) Intrusive (phone call precedes or supplants query).
9) Inappropriate (clips don't match the idea).
10) Careless (faults are mentioned or major gaffe is made).

## A Few Quotes

"All life belongs to you. Do not listen to those who would shut you up into corners of it and tell you that it is only here or there where art inhabits, or to those who would persuade you that this heavenly messenger wings her way outside of life altogether, breathing a superfine air, and turns her head from the truth of things. There is no impression of life, no manner of seeing it and feeling it, to which the plan of the novelist may not offer a place."

--Henry James

"I write to find the words I don't want through subtraction."

--Roland Barthes

"If you would be pungent, be brief; for it is with words as with sunbeams- the more they are condensed, the deeper they burn."

--Robert Southey

"I write not to depict events, but to reawaken our perception."

--unknown

"I desire to speak somewhere without bounds; like a man in a waking moment to men in their waking moments."

--H.D. Thoreau

www.ingramcontent.com/pod-product-compliance
Lightning Source LLC
Chambersburg PA
CBHW022055170626
46808CB00003B/1478